The

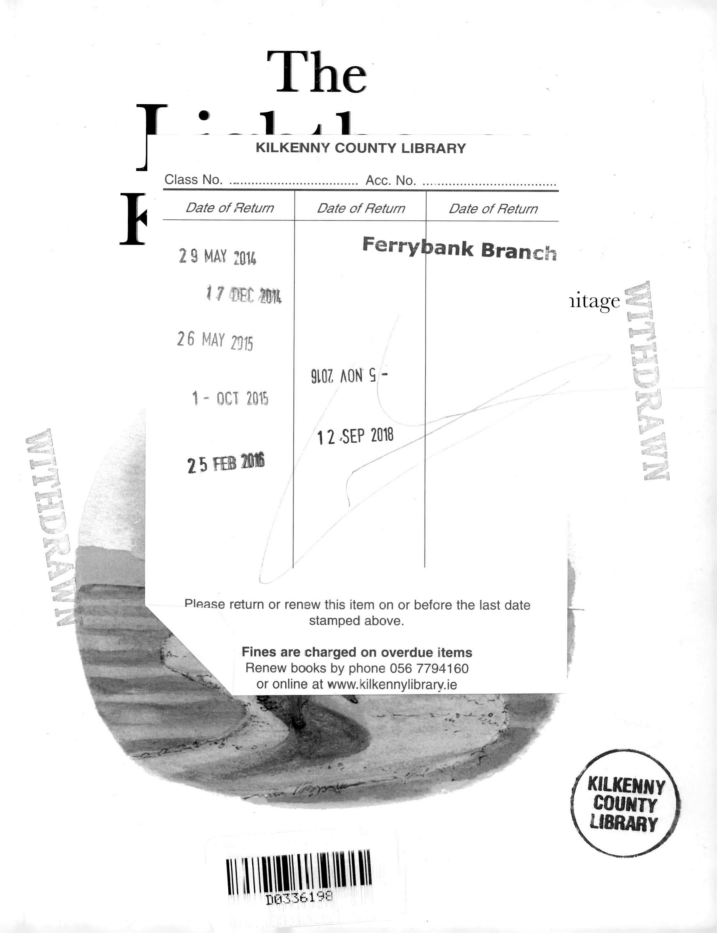

hitage

D0336198

To Harry

First published in 1995 by Scholastic Ltd
This edition first published in 2008 by Scholastic Children's Books
Euston House, 24 Eversholt Street
London NW1 1DB
a division of Scholastic Ltd
www.scholastic.co.uk
London ~ New York ~ Toronto ~ Sydney ~ Auckland
Mexico City ~ New Delhi ~ Hong Kong

Text copyright © 1995 Ronda Armitage
Illustrations copyright © 1995 David Armitage

ISBN 978 1407 10651 9

Hamish lived with Mr and Mrs Grinling
in the little white cottage on the cliffs.
Mr Grinling was the lighthouse keeper.

Some days Hamish went
to work with Mr Grinling.
He liked to help in
the lighthouse.

When visitors came Hamish would
show them round.
"What a magnificent cat!"
they would exclaim.
"Hamish, King of the Lighthouse."

Some days Hamish worked with Mrs Grinling. He liked
digging in the garden where she'd planted the seeds.

He also liked to help with the cooking.
"Fish with everything" was Hamish's motto.
"Not in chocolate cake," said Mrs Grinling firmly.

A lot of the time Hamish
liked to sleep. One night when
he was curled up in his favourite
place he heard Mr and Mrs
Grinling talking.

Hamish's
Breakfast.

Herbert's
Lunch.

HAMISH

PEACH
SURPRISE

"They were there again today," said Mr Grinling, "scampering and squeaking. The Inspector of Lighthouses is coming next week and he says mice might eat the wiring."

"What about Hamish?" asked Mrs Grinling. "He might catch them for you."
Mr Grinling chuckled.
"Our Hamish chase mice? Really, Mrs G, he's much too plump and well fed."
"He might be persuaded if he wasn't quite so well fed," said Mrs Grinling. "He might chase mice if he didn't have any breakfast before he went to the lighthouse."

"You mean starve him," whispered Mr Grinling.
"Sh, Mrs G, he'll be upset if he hears you."
Hamish *was* upset, very upset.
"No breakfast," she'd said.
"Starve him," he'd said.

"Well, my quivering ginger whiskers," he thought,
"We'll see about that.
Nobody starves the lighthouse cat."

"If they don't love me any more I'll go somewhere else to live."
Early next morning Hamish left home.

As he made his way to the village he met all kinds of strange creatures. Some wanted to chase him and some wanted to play.

He was delighted when he smelt a house.
"Mm, fish," sniffed Hamish, "probably shark."

"It's dark in here!"

Oh dear!!

Silly cat!!

222...

Hmm... Shark's fin soup...

A spot of breakfast, I think...

"Look, Mum," called the little boy, "there's an enormous cat at our door. I think he's hungry, can we feed him?"

Hamish liked the breakfast they gave him. He liked the big children. They played hide and seek and chase the mouse with him.

He didn't like the baby. It rolled on him and squashed his ears.

"Not bad though," thought Hamish
as he jumped up to sleep beside
the stove. "I like this house,
I think I'll stay."

"What's this?" exclaimed the mother.
"A cat who jumps on benches,
a scavenging cat. Not in this house.
Scat cat," she said, "out you go!"

And she shut the door behind him.

"Well, my quivering ginger whiskers,"
thought Hamish,
"We'll see about that.
Nobody shouts at this lighthouse cat."

And he stalked off down the road.

A tabby kitten dropped
on him from a tree.

"Play with me and you
can share my dinner."

Hamish liked the dinner so much that he forgot to share.

The kitten swung on his tail.
"Play with me and you can sleep in my bed."

Hamish slept in the bed but he was so large there was no room for the kitten.

"Who's your ginger friend?" asked the old man. The kitten hissed at Hamish. He wasn't a friend, he didn't share.

But Hamish wanted to stay.
He liked the dinner
and he liked the bed.

"I'll show them how clever I am,"
he thought. "I'll make them
look at me."

But the old man and the
kitten took no notice.
They snored and
purred together.

"Well, my quivering ginger whiskers,"
Hamish glared,
"We'll see about that.
Nobody ignores the lighthouse cat."

But he didn't stay grumpy for long. The sun warmed his orange whiskers and the smell of warm mouse tickled his nose.

It was nearly dark when Hamish found the yard. He looked around. "This is no place for a lighthouse cat. Probably mice, possibly rats, maybe. . ."

"CATS!"
They were not pleased to see Hamish.
"Who invited you?" snarled a tattered grey cat.
"This is our place, we don't like strangers," hissed the
one-eyed black.

"Skedaddle mush, beat it! You don't belong here."

Hamish skedaddled, right to the top of the tallest tree.

"Well, my quivering ginger whiskers," he puffed,
"We'll see about that.
Nobody snarls at the lighthouse cat."

He peered over the branches. The cats' eyes gleamed below.

"Perhaps I'll just stay here for a while," thought Hamish.

The lights of the village blinked around him. Far away another
light flashed.
Hamish sat up. "My lighthouse!"
He thought about Mr and Mrs Grinling.
He thought about the little white cottage.
The leaves of the trees rustled and the tree began to sway.
"It's time to go home," thought Hamish.

He looked down the tree again. It was too dark to see the
ground any more.

"I don't like going down,"
thought Hamish. "I CAN'T
go down."
"I want to go home!"

He yeowled and yeowled but nobody heard him. Then the thunder rumbled and the rain poured down.

He yeowled again, but still nobody heard him. After a while the rain stopped and a soggy, sad, ginger cat went to sleep.

Mrs Grinling heard the thunder too.

"Oh, my poor Hamish," she cried to Mr Grinling. "Where is he? He'll be so frightened."

"There, there, my dear," soothed Mr Grinling. "You know our Hamish, he's a clever cat. He'll be snug and warm or I'll eat my hat."

Next morning Mrs Grinling was up very early. There was no sign of Hamish.

"I'm going out to search for him," she said to Mr Grinling. "He might be hurt."

Before she left she did some cooking. Then she set off for the village on her bike.

Round and round and up and down she cycled. Every now and then she would stop and take something out of the basket.

Three seagulls arrived at a
very tall tree near the village.
They flew round it, squawking.

"What a caterwauling," exclaimed Mrs Grinling. "What have
they seen in that tree?"

Three seagulls woke
Hamish with their
noise. He meowed.

"Hamish," called Mrs Grinling.
He looked down. His whiskers quivered.
"I know that smell."
His nose nearly fell off his face.

It was his favourite dinner, Star-gazy Pie. Mrs Grinling
had cooked it specially. They weren't going to starve him
after all.

He meowed and meowed. "You foolish cat," said Mrs Grinling fondly,
"I'll come up and get you."

She put the Star-gazy
Pie in the basket and
climbed to the top
of the tree.

Hamish was so excited that
he fell on to the pie. Mrs Grinling
lowered the basket to the ground.

Mr Grinling was delighted to see Hamish home again.
"Just in time too," he said. "Please, Hamish, I need your help.
If Mrs Grinling cooks you another Star-gazy Pie could you
persuade the mice to find a new home?"
Hamish meowed.

Next morning Hamish and
Mr Grinling rowed out to
the lighthouse.

While Mr Grinling worked, Hamish visited the mice.

When the Inspector of Lighthouses visited there were no mice
scampering or squeaking.
Mr Grinling was very happy. He patted Hamish fondly.
"A great mouse chaser," he said.

The mice were very happy. They nibbled some crumbs
and tried not to squeak.

Hamish was very happy. He stretched out beside the stove.

"Well, my quivering ginger whiskers," he thought,
"He's right about that.
I'm the cleverest, I'm the greatest,
I'm the lighthouse cat."